Caboose
By
Jeremy M. Donger

Jeremy M. Donger

Caboose
By
Jeremy M. Donger

Library of Congress Control Number: 2015940526

Caboose
By
Jeremy M. Donger

One

She met me at 11:53 A.M. at an airport fifty miles away from her home base. She said she had a place for me to stay where I could shoot a video.

In her GMC Envoy we speed up the narrow mountain roads. She took the gravely dirt road too fast. She skidded on the road with a drop cliff on the left, and a fallen tree was obscuring the road. She pressed hard on the brake pedal and skidded sideways, and I hunched in the passenger's seat expecting the GMC to flip and roll. But we slid to the fallen tree within inches and a big pile of rocks blocked us from rolling over tumbling to our deaths. The engine was dead.

"What luck!" Eloisa Parker shouted.

The engine made hissing noises. A crow laughed at us. A lizard hid behind a rock.

"End of the road?"

"Gracious no Mr. Hilton. We can foot it from here. I believe it's a half mile. I haven't been up here in years."

"How about the gear?"

"It didn't look like it is very much stuff. You might as well bring it. Perhaps you could play Superman and lift the vehicle off the ground and place it on the other side and we could drive on the road."

"I better go find a phone booth to change in."

"Now you're thinking."

We smiled.

I lifted my pack out of the car and we hiked over the tree. The road was steep and the curves were dangerous.

She hiked up the gravel road in leather boots, a red suit skirt, and a grass hat. There was no wind and the sun made the walking hot and scorching.

From meeting her I had been trying to figure her out. She was a rip-bodied blond of about thirty with narrow hips. She had a lot of self respect, and a way of handling herself. She would have looked to fit in a home on Park Avenue and Fifty something in the high style on a Wednesday afternoon donning a fantastic hat.

I stopped and put my pack down and took off my suit coat.

"Now you're thinking," she said pulling hers and laying it on the ground. "Just in case we don't make it, we'll make love right here."

She continued undressing. Her suit skirt was spread on the ground, revealing a narrow waist. Her body was truly an earth shaking event, to be signaled by rare wine and silk sheets but we were high up a trail and I unbuckled my pants, pulling my shirt and underwear and my love muscle was erect before her as she pulled her bra off. She and I stepped nearer and she lowered on her knees and took me in her mouth. Her tongue massaged my member like a professional. She held my body at the hips as she took each inch of my shaft in her mouth as she could fit in. A sigh escaped my lips as the warmth of her glands touched my penis and I held her head as it moved back and forth on my member. She slurped and swallowed each inch of me, sucking my flesh to licking my shaft and encasing my length till I creamed a hot spurt of goo in her mouth. She was gladder to taste my hot love juice in her mouth and swallowing; the sperm reaching her tonsils and going in to her stomach.

"Now that your ding dong has had a great slurping, it is ready for a massage from my slope hole," she murmured turning on her knees.

She held her back straight as she pulled me to her ass an I entered her love canal.

I increased my pace and fucked her rougher making her scream loudly.

This was truly an earth-shaking event. Never had I had sex on the mountains with a hot girl ready to fuck like there was no tomorrow which there was a chance we may not live to tomorrow.

The pale skin of her back shone brightly in the sunshine as I gripped her ass thrusting long dick into her pussy hole.

This was the greatest sex I ever had.

The road ended at a large house. It was on an acre of level ground, a rocky shelf mid-way of the way up the mountain side. The house was of marble, fifty feet square, with a roof at eighty degree angle. There was an open shed beside it containing power tools, and a Cadillac jeep.

I followed her up onto the veranda and she pried a key out the small pocket of her skirt and unlocked the big metallic door.

"This is the sitting room. That fireplace heats beautifully in the winter.

Kitchen through there with vintage appliances. Cast iron stove. There's a spring in the back and an indoor pool. The water is piped into the house from a spring out back. Hot water and cold water. Fresh water. The boiler room is in the basement. I assume you saw the Cadillac jeep in the shed. It should have a full tank of gas and a personal fuel station and pump around back. There are some clothes in that closet there. I think you could make do."

I put my gear on the lounge sofa.

I sat on a stool nearby.

"This house is a perfect place to shoot a video."

"It is a lovely home; the perfect getaway."

She sat on a leather cushion of the sitting stool. She had put her suit coat on a hanger behind the door and her hat. Her bosom was perspiring from our union and the hike.

"Is there an air conditioner in this place?"

"There is. I'll go turn it on."

She returned in less clothing than before, in a swimsuit.

"Do you swim Mr. Hilton? There is swimwear in that closet."

"I swim. That will be refreshing."

I made my way to the closet and found swimming trunks. She took a stool as I dressed.

"My husband doesn't know you're here. He'll think I'm having an affair with another man. I'm in love with another man anyway and he doesn't want to give me the divorce."

"Love is a mystery."

"Yes, love is one great mystery. How long does love last is another mystery. I shouldn't bring my status into this. The house is for rent as long as you would like. We'll discuss the price after I get a swim."

"Do you need help Mrs. Parker?"

"You couldn't begin to believe how much help. I don't want to bore you with my situation Mr. Hilton."

"If you need to talk about it, please do. Maybe we could come up with something."

Mrs. Parker took in a deep breath.

"My father was Archie Wallace. That doesn't mean anything to you, I figure. But he is a man to remember around here. I was his only daughter and child. My mother died three years after I was born. He died twenty three years ago, when I was thirteen. He was thirty-nine. His closest and dear friend was Prentice Parker. Prentice was forty when daddy died. The will named Prentice the executioner. He took over everything in the will. He was kind and generous. I went to school in England, Mr. Hilton. After I graduated in England, I went to work in Vermont, on a clothing line. I was on a wealthy allowance. I was twenty three. Cupid shot his arrow and I fell in love with a married man. I was his mistress. We ran away together on expensive cruises. It was a ghastly mistake. In Paris he had a change of heart and went savaging back to his loving wife. I stayed in Paris, for almost two years. I drank too much and did some foolish things like get pregnant and had an abortion. Then I fell ill. Then Prentice came over. He took me to London and stayed with me till I recovered in health. I needed emotional support, love and affection. Prentice and I were married in London. We honeymooned there, eight years ago. He's sixty-three now. Up until two years ago, life was comfortable as a pillow. Prentice is successful and rich and a tough minded individual. It was a first marriage for me and him. We did not have children because of me. Two years ago I fell in love again with another man. I figured Prentice would be reasonable and find another woman to love. He hasn't. I decided to leave him. I thought I'd get the money my father left me and leave him and move on. I were getting the allowance which I thought was from the interest the estate held in trust for me. There were several trust funds. I had been receiving two thousand dollars a month since I was twenty-one and spending it with no worries. Prentice is the executioner as I told you. I asked him for an accounting and he laughed at me. I hate when I get laughed at. Prentice said the estate of my father had been dry years ago, and that he had continued my allowance on his own accord at his expense. I demanded to see the figures for my sake. He said they would not mean anything to me if I did see them. He said my father made foolish investments, and that the estate money ran dry when we were married in London."

Sitting there in her swimsuit, and her bikini were hunching on the side of her love canal, I were following her cunt like the paparazzi. Mrs. Parker stood and made her way to me with the stool. I rammed my penis in her once.

To ram my meat in her again were on my thought of mind. But I focused on her lips. Then her breasts. Then her lips.

"You married a man over twenty years your age because you needed emotional support, love and affection. You really married him for the money."

"I married him for the money. Mr. Hilton, my father was rich! He put what he had in his will to another man and not his flesh and blood daughter. At the time he died the papers said that his estate, before taxes were exempted, was worth over nine million dollars. It couldn't be gone as Prentice speaks. I think my husband has taken the money and is covering it up," she said and touched my hand.

"Mrs. Parker, I think you need a lawyer and an accountant for your situation."

"Let me relay to you the facts of life. Nine miles down the mountain is the city of Las Vegas. In the city is the Las Vegas State Bank and trust company. Prentice is the city and the county and the bank, and he is many other things; an entrepreneur. My husband goes on executive trips with other men who run the casinos and the entire state of Nevada. He sits at the casinos and plays slot machines and poker with them. I am being treated like a little kid, as if this was a temper tantrum and I go to a corner or no sugar pixies. I'm supposed to be a pretty young woman like Snow White and not get my dress dirty."

"Did you go to a lawyer?"

"I could not find a lawyer in Clark County who wasn't scared. I found a lawyer in Nye County. He nudged around for about two months. He said my husband had to give his stewardship to a probate judge, file reports with courts, I guess because I was a minor. He made eight reports after daddy died, and nine years later, and thirteen years later. That was a final report, four years ago, filing the estate was exhausted. The judge was murdered. Three years ago a new court house was built and the files were not indexed, and there is no way of for sure the files exist. The lawyer Prentice used was murdered, and nobody knows where his files and records went. To get a copy of the tax statement filed with the federal government twenty years ago, identify the assets, and trace them through public records of sales and so forth, he would have to begin from the other end, and build up a case that some kind of laundry had been going on. I would then have to bring action against my husband. Even if we got something to go on, he said Prentice could stall for four or three years before we could ever get it to court. Meanwhile, my allowance has been cut off until I, come to my senses. He kisses me and tells me to forget this nonsense like I'm Cinderella telling me the glass slipper doesn't fit."

"Perhaps Mrs. Parker, the estate wasn't big as you thought it was."

"My father loved land. I can show you one of the pieces he owned next to a casino. Now it's got a casino on it, a shopping plaza, exquisite diner and three hundred hotel resorts. The lawyer checked it out at the County Clerk's office, and it wasn't sold to pay estate taxes. The records show it was sold forty three months ago to something called the Index Commercial Incorporation. The records in the state capital show that Index lasted four years three months and collapsed like an elderly woman with a pacemaker, with no panic button. My father owned this area right here, also. Thirteen thousand acres. Prentice knew I loved this place. He gave me the deed to part of it, ten thousand acres, for my anniversary seven years ago. He said he bought it back from the buyers. Eight months ago I looked into the idea of selling it, but Prentice name is on the deed too, and I can't. The estate was swindled from me, by my husband Prentice. There has to be a way of making him make restitution. A way of taking me seriously. Because I am serious. I want a divorce, I want to marry Carl Thomson, and I want my money."

"Carl Thomson is your new love, I assume."

"Carl is not rich, and not poor. He's a professor at the University of Nevada Las Vegas. The legislator controls the university. Prentice has friends at the university. According to Prentice, the day I leave him, Carl Thomas gets booted out with small chances of getting a job elsewhere. I've been reduced to being a hostage in my marriage, Mr. Hilton."

"A smart woman can make a man glad to be rid of her."

"I have been a total hag for months and he laughs at me. Prentice says I'll get over it. He's very ardent. I have not let him touch me and that does not seem to bother him either. Maybe he has another woman. He is so horribly sure I will pass this 'temper tantrum', and be his lovely bride again. Prentice said once I began acting like his wife again we can return to the way things were. I had to sell jewelry to pay the lawyer and your plane ticket."

"I do not see how there is anything which can be done other than find a way of blackmail."

"Mr. Hilton, I want to be realistic about this situation. Blackmail is what I had in mind. I've scaled my wants. I want him convinced he should let me go. My only other option is sit around and wait for him to die and I am not great at role playing. And he is a healthy man. Killing him would be very suspicious."

"You could just take off with this Carl."

She made an unhappy face. "I threaten that I would. He said he would never divorce me for deserting him. He said he would hire people to find me and bring me back. And those people would give Carl a beating for wife-stealing. Carl isn't Hulk Hogan or Iron Man or the Incredible Hulk. No. Prentice has to want to divorce me and let me go."

She stood up and her bra buddy popped out her bikini top and she pulled her bikini bottom over her cunt. She had a lot of vitality, a lot of bounce in her boobs and buttocks. A pretty woman with no money, she did not look like the kind you can quell and keep humble. She was like a bumble bee; busy body. She led me through a hall to the in ground indoor swimming pool. The pool was a twenty five yard long pool with a diving board.

"Why would your husband take your money?" I asked as if greed was not involved somehow.

She climbed the board and dove in.

There was a splash.

She came up from the water palming her blond hair back with both hands.

"I think I know why. I heard rumors. When I was about fourteen, he had some very bad years. He was always bold in a business way. I figure he got too bold an overextended himself in too many directions, so when things began going sour for him, he didn't have enough money to move around. So he had to dig into mine to save his caboose. Perhaps he thought he would pay it back, but he had to dip in more, and do a lot of shifty work before he could fill the barrel and reseal. I guess by then it seemed logistic to close out the estate rather than try to pack it back. And the best way to cover it all up was to marry me. When he saw his chance to marry me, he capitalized on the opportunity. I don't think he ever really want to be married to me."

I knifed in the pool behind her on the board.

I came up wiping my face with my hand.

"He saw a perfect opportunity to cover his tracks and get a pretty woman. And you made it easier for him because you were money hungry," I said.

"He isn't that sort of guy. He had to marry me to protect him. And I had to put my bid in on my inheritance."

"Don't defend him. Had you not married him and hired a lawyer sooner, you wouldn't be having this dilemma."

"If you are meaning my shady marriage was spongy, it was. But during the years it seemed pretty good, I never did have the status of a wife. He did not change his way of life or even seem to take me seriously. We were each a tool in the marriage. I'll race you to the other end."

"You're on."

I was a great swimmer. It was a tight finish to the end. I beat her by inches.

"Your marriage to Prentice was more of a marriage of convenience yet you did not know he squandered the money, or hid the money. I don't see where you have any approach to this. Does he have any secrets or scams you are aware of?"

"None which I know of other than this. He didn't pull these things like he has a machine to make him invisible. I'm sure he'd made enemies. Somebody he must have made an enemy has enough to put pressure on him. And I don't think Prentice is confident about this enough as he would like me to believe. I guess it would look bad if the newspapers picked it up-Prentice Parker's wife demanding an account of what and where is her father's money. I figure he maybe was worried I had squirreled away some of my allowance."

"Why do you think that?" I asked turning to her and she swam to me with an answer.

"I had a nice attractive Japanese maid, Mayumi Jade for four years. She quit about eight months ago. A man went to her and questioned her for hours, mostly about my personal finances, how much I spent an on what. He claimed to be an account of some sort. Afterwards she worried about it for about a month and then came and told me. That happened just three months ago. I had an unusual relationship with Mayumi. I and Mayumi confided in each other almost like sisters. She was dear to me."

"That does not sound like an unusual relationship between a lady and their maid. She is always there and she is another female which may understand your emotions."

"I guess it was not unusual. Do you think Prentice was doing the maid?"

"That's what you should ask him, not me."

"Maybe he was doing the maid."

"Perhaps he was boning the maid and the guy who was the suppose accountant were really there to see how much of the things Prentice bought her and she saved. Your husband did not win the Mr. Universe contest. And you think that because your husband might be worried, he might be susceptible to some kind of pressure to let you go."

"He was a piece of slime for his greater self. If I knew what to do, I would have tried to do it myself, Mr. Hilton. I hired a guy to find out about other women. I guess the guy got clumsy. The police threw him in jail for stalking. Two days he was in jail and he gave up the investigation."

"I just don't know how I could be of help to you," I said.

"You can help me Mr. Hilton," she said seductively and pulled her bikini off and pressed her lips against mine.

My hands slide around her narrow hips to her bottom to her slit where I fingered her and her clit. She wound her legs around my torso as I enter her. The water was helpful as I held her ass pivoting into her cunt.

Our union was divine. She let go of her frustrations with her husband through our union. I spasms in her. She orgasms. The pool needed cleaning.

Globs of sperm and pussy cum floated to the top of the pool.

She made her way out the pool to the glass windows. She opened the glass door. I got out of the pool and stood near her. The indoor pool overlooked the city below. The mountainous hills around us were gray-brown, with little patches of green trees and bushes. She pointed down below. The land cascaded down and flattened out to the view of the city. To the right were the spring and trees and more mountain tops. She pointed to the valley below about three miles away. I could make out casinos and hotels. She stood half facing me.

"I'm thirty six years old, Mr. Hilton. In a way, I'm grateful to him. But I want out of this marriage. I'm a captive princess, and this and that is the kingdom down there. Prentice is the king. I can have a little freedom of motion, as long as I take a carriage back to the kingdom before nightfall. Lame, I guess. When you are in love you get some romantic images and I'm not too ancient to cry myself to sleep. I must have some help."

She was a whore and she was screwed. Not only from me because we did screw in the pool; from her father and her husband.

She stood at my left, half turned to face me, the sun heat of the day misting her breasts and thighs. Mrs. Parker wanted an answer. And I frowned in silence, searching for the words to tell her that she's screwed. Wait till he's dead or plot his murder.

I couldn't tell her she's screwed. I'll lead her on making suggestions and slang dick in her again.

Suddenly she pulled backward. She went with her head tilted back, and she landed a meter from the pool. The noise that started the fall was curiously ugly. It was the sound of impact like someone slicing a corn of cob on a cutting board. She lay without twitch, without sound, totally still with a hole in her head and a puddle of blood began surrounding her head. I heard the distant ringing bark of a heavy riffle, an echoing in the pool house from the open glass door.

A sniper was out there and I ran very fast and a random pattern to the house away from the windows. I watched the windows, saw nothing, and heard nothing. The princess is no longer held captive. I swallowed the gagging lump that was the clear visual memory of the wet hole punched in her head.

I peered from the doorway at her lifeless body. Dear Mrs. Parker was dead before she knew what happened. I had to settle myself down and keep my ears and eyes open for footsteps and gunshots. Maybe the killer was circling the house and would come through the front door. I had to get out of there. I remembered the Cadillac in the shed. The road was blocked off down the road we came, but it was a better idea than going out there on foot with a sniper, or staying in here not knowing if he had a key to the house, or figuring how many exits this place had.

I quickly dressed and pulled out my iPhone to dial for help. There was no signal. I didn't know specifically where her house was located anyway.

I search the house quickly for the keys. The leather cushion stool still bore that imprint of that round bottom. I saw her suit skirt hung behind the door. Her leather purse was hanging on the back of a bedroom door. I found one hundred and thirty-nine dollars in it and no keys. I took the one hundred and thirty-nine. She was dead. She wasn't going to need the cash any more. Her iPhone was there with her on the screen saver with a casino in the background. I grabbed my gear, took three deep breaths, and then went running for the shed to the sports utility vehicle. Maybe I could hot wire it. The door was unlocked and I kept my head low. I opened the glove box. No keys were in site. I pulled the sun visor and the keys fell in my lap. I quickly put the key in the ignition, put the Cadillac in gear, and put the pedal to the metal.

There was no trail in back. My only way was down. I speed down the same road we hiked up searching for a detour somewhere on the gravely road.

There was none. I drove around the curb where the road block was, and there was none. The tree was dragged to the side and the GMC was gone. Whoever killed Mrs. Parker were in a vehicle and I was not about to stop and look for tire marks. I kept driving fast as I could on the mountainous roads.

One wrong turn and I'll be tumbling to my death.

Caboose

If the killer cleared the pathway, why did he take the GMC and where did he take the Envoy?

I pushed that out my mind and drove for my life.

Two

Three or two miles down the road was the metal gate I had opened and closed again when Mrs. Parker had driven the Envoy through. Why tumble the tree on the road? To make her leave the GMC there and walk then kill her? So somebody could steal the vehicle? Why?

I ran out of answers and continued driving on down the mountain. I thought how merciless it is to kill a provocative woman with a pretty face and a generous slope hole. They are not supposed to be killed like that. No one is suppose to render useless all that sweet pale skin and membrane.

But dead she was, and dead on arrival she will be. I headed down the trail and at last I came to the vaguely remembered crossroads, to a diner. A man stood in the inside of the diner behind the cash register.

I went into the diner. A narrow hip girl in a red apron sat at a table reading the

Casino Gazette. She got up slowly when I walked in. She had enormous breasts I would not mind suckling and squeezing and she looked like Lindsay Logan.

"I need to use the phone."

She did not say a word. She looked like she was undressing me with her eyes. As I had already undressed her with my eyes when I seen her big breasts. She pointed to the phone.

"What is the name of this place? So I can give someone directions."

"Larry's at Casino Wits."

I got out two quarters and looked in front of the book. Police emergency, dial 555-1234.

"Las Vegas sheriff's department. Deputy Slayer."

"I'm at Larry's place at Casino Wits. I want to report a murder and a theft of a motor vehicle."

"Did it happen there?"

"No. But I can take you to the place it did happen."

"What is your name Sir?"

"Hilton. Martin Hilton." I was aware of the rigid attention of the big boob babe behind me.

"I can have a car there in about twenty minutes. You wait there. Do you have a description of the stolen vehicle Mr. Hilton?"

"It is a red GMC Envoy. Local tags."

"Do you know the tag number?"

"No."

"Do you know the driver?"

"I have the slightest idea."

"Where exactly did it happen?"

"It happened in the mountain hills about seven or eight miles from here. I drove out so it happened about twenty minutes ago."

"Who was hurt?"

"A woman by the name of Mrs. Eloisa Parker. She was murdered."

"Mrs. Parker! Goodness gracious! You wait right there!"

I put the receiver in the cradle. The big boob babe looked adoringly at me.

"Well how about that!" she said. "Son of a gun! How about a Mountain Dew?"

"Sure."

"Do you want a glass or no glass?"

"No glass."

"Hey, what happened to Mrs. Parker? Who killed her?"

"Do you know her?"

"Who doesn't know Mrs. Parker? Mrs. Parker ate here lots of time. Her husband Prentice owned half of this county. She was a whore and a money grubber. Who killed her?"

"I better let the police do the questioning."

She banged the Mountain Dew down in front of me and walked away. I heard her jabbering at the man who was behind the cash register. They both came back with curious eyes. He was tan and had a Las Vegas vibe to him like a card shark. He looked at me like I won a big poker game and he was leeching for a celebration handout. "That woman is dead for sure, huh?"

They both looked at me like I brought them word of a UFO with cargo of diamonds.

"I take it you're not from around here because I never seen you, and you don't know who Mrs. Parker is. She was the daughter of Archie Wallace. My daddy worked for Mr. Wallace a time. Mr. Wallace didn't marry until he was thirty one. Eloisa was his only legal child, but you can bet a horse's ass there is about thirty or forty people running around her with his blue eyes. Mr. Wallace was kind to many folks, if you get my drift. Mr. Wallace and Mr. Parker, they used to run together. My father said when Prentice married the Wallace daughter; he bet Archie were turning in his grave. Who killed her Sir?" the big breasts babe asked.

"I'm a stranger around this area."

A car pulled up and someone gave the siren a short blare so that it made a growl.

We went out of the diner. It was a white Chevy Caprice with Las Vegas Sheriff on the door. A man in uniform stepped out. He wore a khaki uniform and silver badge and a gun belt.

"Lira, Larry," the skinny bald man said.

"Hi, Wheeler."

Wheeler ringed his belt with his hands, indicating me with a nod of the head and said, "I assume you heard him on the phone, didn't you? You and Lira?"

"I sure did. And if it isn't a shocking thing--"

"Larry, you or Lira better keep shut about this till we know what's going on."

"We'll keep quite but if the Associated Press comes asking questions, we won't hesitate to get free publicity. This is the story of the century around here."

"Don't go running your guns till we know what's what." He turned to me and said, "Mr. Hilton?"

"Martin Hilton."

"I'm Harry Wheeler. The Sheriff will be right along. We'll wait for him. He'll ask the questions. Here he comes," Wheeler said. An identical Chevy came at high speed, swerved in and stopped in a pillar of dust.

The Sheriff stepped out of the car. He was older than the deputy about eight years. He had broad shoulders, a round jaw, sagging neck, the look of an obese guy who lost a lot of weight. He wore a star on his uniform.

"Wheeler?" he said.

"I haven't asked Mr. Hilton here any questions, so you know as much right now as I do."

"Follow us on up," the Sheriff said.

I got in with the Sheriff in the passenger seat. His name was Fickle.

"Where did it happen at Mr. Hilton?"

"Go straight up the hill about four miles and there is a gate..."

"To the house with the pool, huh? I know the spot. Who shot Mrs. Parker?"

"My first guess is the husband shot her or hired a sniper. The bullet hit her in the head and she died in seconds. I left her where she were and ran for my life. I didn't see anybody. I heard the rifle shot ringing in my ear."

"When did the shooting happen?"

"I didn't look at my Rolex. I estimate now, more than a half hour ago. I guess at two twenty."

"The road leads to her home."

"There was a fallen tree in the road when we came up. She left the key in the Envoy. I drove down the same road and the fallen tree was pulled to the side and the GMC gone."

34

We had come to the big gate. The deputy opened the gate, we drove through.

He closed the gate and we continued up the mountain.

"Where do you fit in to this scenario Mr. Hilton?"

"I'm a producer. Mrs. Parker was a friend of a friend. Anita Nelson. Mrs. Nelson, a widow, a friend of Eloisa Parker. A while back she visited Eloisa. I've wanted a place where I could complete a project; keep expenses down at the same time. Anita suggested I could use the house Mrs. Parker owned with the pool. And if I'd like, I could go to the casinos and maybe have fun. Las Vegas is a show attraction. So I got in touch with Mrs. Parker and she agreed to loan it to me. I flew in around 11:53 A.M. to the house. R'ss. Parker showed me the house. It was agreeable to both of us with the use of the Cadillac I was driving. She wanted a swim. And all of sudden, standing at the pool door the slug knocked her down dead."

We came to the house. The house was locked. But the pool door leading outside was able to be pried open easily.

"What type of project are you working on Mr. Hilton?" the Sheriff asked.

"I am shooting a music video for a client. It would have been a great place to work."

Once the pool door was open, I was shocked. The Sheriff and his deputy stared at me. I felt my mouth stretch in a foolish grin. "The body was right here."

There was no dead body. There was no puddle of blood.

I knew that I saw the bullet hole in her head. I sat on my heels next to where her body went down. They stared at me skeptically. The Sheriff Fickle and Deputy Wheeler shrugged and began to feel around where her body had laid.

"Well she changed into her swimsuit."

We went into the house. The door was unlocked.

The house had a flavor of being empty for months. Her suit skirt, hat and purse were gone.

"Now what in crap is going on?" Fickle said irritably.

I described what Mrs. Parker was wearing. I described her sports utility

Caboose

vehicle. I told them where the bullet had hit
her and the puddle of blood and where her
body feel.

They both stared at me.

They went out. I heard Wheeler
laughing at me. Fickle stood and said, "This
was a fool idea, Mr. Hilton."

"What are you talking about?"

"This charade. That woman has been
threatening to leave her husband Prentice
for the longest. And now she concocted you
into the scenario and found the way to run
off with that professor Carl. She's been after
her old man for months to divorce her and
turn her loose to go with Carl. Prentice has
been kidding around Las Vegas the gal has
got the trots. She'll get over it and come
running straight back to Prentice. She
knows well off she won't get very far
without her husband Prentice. And Prentice
will give her a good whipping for running
off with a fool like Carl to get involved
with a married woman. She's just got a little
boredom Mr. Hilton and the hot pants.
She's been promiscuous in the past. She'll
learn soon enough not to go trotting behind
every man which smiles at her. Don't

worry. She'll come crawling back sooner or later. Carl is not exactly some big CEO type coon."

"Shouldn't we go looking for her?"

"And go searching all over Las Vegas and find them two shacked in a hotel? You did good Mr. Hilton. You almost had me believing somebody did her in. This is the sort of thing I hear her father used to pull, only better. I guess it runs in the family. Father like daughter, huh?"

"She was murdered. I saw her body. I saw blood dripping from her head. I heard the high powered riffle rip a whole in her head."

"Let me tell you something Mr. Hilton. Mrs. Parker has foolish friends who would try prying her loose from Prentice. That GMC is stuffed in a parking lot someplace. Mrs. Parker and that nutty professor are high-tailing it out of here by now to their romantic getaway. She's scared of Prentice and wants a head start. If we thought her dead, it would give her another week or two to get hid better and get the loving she's aching for from that professor of hers. Soon as I get the SUV, I get in touch with

Prentice and he'll have her back here within the week. And she'll be eating off high places when Prentice gives her a welting with her hot bottom. What are you the actor friend?"

"No. If that was the plan, where is the nice trimming huh?"

"Trimming?"

"The icing on the cake--Where is the fake blood. Why is there no sign or something to make it look better like she was dead?"

"There is no fake blood because there is need of a fake body. And with a fake body, you know she's not dead."

"I know I saw her body go down Sheriff."

"The next time I see Mrs. Parker, I'll tell her you gave it a good try Mr. Hilton."

"Why not get the forensics team in here and turn them loose?"

"You never give up do you? There's no need for forensics. We'll have a lead on them before sunrise. Prentice will have a long arm stretched out from here to the other side of the globe. Let's get out of here."

We went out into the dense sunlight of September, soon to fall behind Spring Mountain.

"The way I picture it, Prentice gave her a long range and she was a young hot woman who didn't want to settle down from the first place. The fancy got to her."

Everybody seemed so certain of everything. We trudged back to the cars.

Fickle sent Deputy Wheeler back on patrol. He started to get his communications a phone link to Prentice and did otherwise. "There are too many people with scanners. They'll laugh this one up today," he explained to me in the car down the hill.

"If I were to guess the weapon, I would say a .40 caliber. It has great velocity and accuracy that will leave a clean entrance wound."

"For crying out loud, Hilton this is Las Vegas! There could be any amount of people with that much gun!"

"I guess it would. But you can at least take a look into things. What if she was murdered?"

"There would be a body."

"There wouldn't be a body because it will look like she ran off with this Carl fellow. Think about. It will be the perfect cover," I said.

I had a point and he knew it. Whether he showed it, he knew it.

"I'll give Mr. Parker a mention. I'm sure she just ran away with Carl. Nobody wants to hurt a pretty blond. At least not the wife of Mr. Parker," Fickle said.

"Thank you Sheriff."

"Now about that Cadillac--I think it is best Mr. Parker knows where that is at. You'll need to clear that with him, Mr. Hilton. Until then I am headed to town."

"I am of in need of my gear in the Cadillac."

"Are you going to stay long Mr. Hilton?"

"I might ask Mr. Parker if I could use that house and the vehicle."

"Don't try to get any frilly than you are."

"What do you mean, Sheriff?"

"He might think you are the new crush his wife has and won't sit pretty."

We came to the diner and I got my gear.

"Could you give me a lift to a decent hotel? Not too dingy and cheap."

"If you could find a cheap hotel here, you have a magic genie."

The sun was gone, but the afterglow cast an orange glow on the buildings.

He pulled into a Super 8 Hotel, said it was clean and reasonable, told me to take it easy, what's in Vegas stays in Vegas, let me out and drove off.

The hotel was a mile from a casino, between a Texaco service station and the Peppermill diner. Across the highway was a Burger King, Taco Bell, and up the line a restaurant from the guy on Master Chef. Ramsay.

An attractive black hair pale skin young woman with red lipstick and narrow hips checked me into number eight.

I went down to room eight. There was a small swimming pool with a high blue fence for privacy beyond the slew of rooms. I had my share of pools today for a swim. Although the right woman like the hotel desk clerk would do this stay some sprucing--skinny dipping and fucking in the pool.

There were two couples in the pool necking. The pool was clean and bare. I checked the mattress and sheets for bed bugs. There were none. I shed my clothes and lay out on the bed.

I had liked Eloisa. She was attractive. Her pleasure paradise was wet. She had pretty skin, narrow hips and a great pair of legs. A man cannot keep from making speculations of her expertise in bed with her promiscuousness.

Maybe I was a chess piece in her scheme. Perhaps this was a rouse and she and her lover were somewhere on the highway or an airplane on their way to a resort where they can stride around nude without anybody sneaking in on them.

So she liked sex and any man who smiled at her she liked, and did. I'm glad I smiled at her. But why go to lengths to get away from her husband? Carl wasn't rich as Prentice Parker, yet he wasn't without either. A man could earn plenty of money in his profession.

She was a pretty blond standing next to me nude at a pool and suddenly she was falling to her death. That sight stayed deeper in me than I would like it to because it was puzzling. There is more to this dilemma than I could think. Maybe her husband got tired of her and had silenced her. Her death was the only way to save his hide and shut her up. What nudged me so was that I saw her limp body. I had thought that I was in the fine tune, but when I learned of her male hopping tendencies, it went together running away with another man not her husband.

One thing nagged at me the most. If it was a murder, why leave the stranger alive? Who was aware I was coming? And whether it was a charade, there still was a loose end. I seen her fall and she wouldn't have so much of a head start to hide away with Carl Thomson. This could become a very dangerous climate. I can't take any solo strolls through Las Vegas, drink or eat anything that doesn't come in a plastic wrapper. I should not sit with my back turned to a window and I should watch the hands of strangers and everybody is a stranger around here.

That's high paranoia.

I had a plane ticket out of here courteous of Mrs. Parker. I could make it out of here on a plane if the plane is not high jacked by terrorists waving box cutters, and the passengers are not scared to fight back. I can't jump the terrorists solo and render the terrorists inoperable. I can grab a parachute, jump off the plane, save myself, and let everyone else die on the plane because they're scared of a guy with a box cutter. Or jump off the plane with the inflatable seat cushion. Either or, I'm coming from the plane alive.

I knew I had made up my mind when Mrs. Parker had not come to the house for months. Somebody had known she was coming. And that somebody knew I was with her. Did the killer follow her? Did that somebody know who I was? I didn't see the killer.

I went out the hotel room and found the ice machine and fixed a cold drink of water in the plastic wrapped cups the hotels equipped in the room that reads the cups are made from recyclable materials.

She had the feeling she was being followed lately. It seems unlikely she would tell her husband I was coming to stay awhile, if she wanted me to help her against him. Somebody else killed her, but in more scenarios than one, the husband killed her or hired somebody to kill her. Whoever killed her could've stolen the Envoy. He wouldn't have the speed to get from the house and steal the vehicle. He could've taken the vehicle and then come up the mountain and get in position and kill her. He could kill her and clean the house for evidence because the murder was planned. There must be another way to the house, another trail where the killer came from the house.

I lounged against the headboard and tried to make sense out of what happened and who could supply the missing pieces of the puzzle. The lawyer Mrs. Parker hired, whom I don't know his name? I could check the phone listing for lawyers and the sheriff's department for arrests and get his name. Carl Thomson?

Who is nowhere to be found? Mr. Parker? Who will more likely seem cooperative, an offended, and who will really not be cooperative putting false pretexts into action? Mayumi?

My window was open and I wondered why. The hotel room had an air conditioner in the wall. I turned the air conditioner on and closed the window. A couple walked by my window with their kid in hand. I closed the curtains and took a nap.

I awoke to the sounds of a couple fucking in the next room. Her sighs were long and exasperated. The guy was putting it to her right or she was boosting his ego like they do in porno films. Then I remembered I didn't remember seeing a guy go in next door. It were two women. I went next door and knocked on the door. A sexy red hair Caucasian looking female came to the door.

"Yes?"

The female wore a red robe reaching to her knees. I could see the other female laying in the bed under the bed sheet. Her hair was long and black.

Each female had an attractive physique, which were narrow hips, big breasts, sexy legs, pretty faces.

"Can I join you?"

The females peered at each other and at me.

"Come in."

I came in the hotel room and the female closed the door after me and took her robe off.

Her breasts plopped out at me and I immediately suckled them as we guided each other to the bed where her girlfriend lay.

"This is my girlfriend Eliza" she said. "I am Trina and we're sisters."

The sister thing was shocking and was erotic. I like.

They did resemble in facial features and their bodies were one of a kind.

Eliza was big breasts, narrow hips, sexy legs, long black hair. Trina was sexy, almost exotic like with dark eyes, long red hair, narrow hips, sexy legs, and her pussy was clean shaved and pinkish. Eliza's eyes were bright red and her pussy was blood red looking; darker in color, and with bigger flaps, and clean shaved. Both their skin were pretty in complexion; perfect pale skin, smooth and rich like white milk chocolate. Both their areolas were large and dark.

Trina massaged my naked body an Eliza devoured me with her lips kissing me erratically on the mouth and neck. Trina took my man meat in her mouth giving my penis a massage with her tongue coercing the sperm to enter her esophagus.

I came in Trina's mouth and Trina shared my sperm with her sister Eliza kissing her in the mouth.

They licked each other's lips fingering their wet juicy pussies. Then Eliza sat her fetus flaps on my fun stick, her back to me and I began fucking her wet cunt. Trina silenced her moans plopping her juicy cunt in her mouth.

Minutes after Eliza erupted and her vagina fluids flowed on my crotch and thighs and on her ass. Trina licked Eliza's slope hole and my penis of the love juices. Trina had her protein for now. She kneeled on the bed as Eliza licked her pussy from behind and spreading Trina's ass open for my entrance into Trina's love canal. Eliza licked my shaft as I entered into Trina.

These sisters were freaky kinky.

Trina and my body smacked as I boned her ass soft like a pillow while she ate her sister's pussy.

Our undulations put her in trimmers and shutters as she orgasms. My shaft was lathered with thick foam from her spasms.

I love when a woman's liquids foam creamy white on my dick.

I didn't wear a rubber so I spat my liquid pearls in her asshole.

Las Vegas is always a place to visit. I may move here some day when I tire of La La Land. Who could get tired of La La Land, the home of movie stars, producers alike?

Fucking these Las Vegas girls were better than going to the casinos gambling.

I had a though: I could get these women to do the music video for a client. Fuck that!

"Do you girls want to do a sex video?" I asked Trina an Eliza as they lay on each side of me with their nipples erect and their cunt super wet. "I'm a producer and you two sisters are film quality."

Trina an Eliza looked from one to another and smiled.

"Yes," Trina an Eliza agreed.

I recorded our fucking on my iPhone. These high technology phones are mini computers. I can ask my phone questions and get answers. I can type documents on the phone with the word processor. I can connect the phone to a printer and print the document. I can scan a barcode on a product and the price will show on the screen. With my phone I can draw pictures, listen to and download music, and plenty other things a computer could do including watch TV and movies and make movies and videos and upload the videos to the internet on YouTube. I can plug my iPhone into a fifty inch screen 3D TV set and watch the download on a bigger screen. Mobile phones today are the next great invention.

I stayed the night in the hotel room with the women, ordered dinner, an ordered lunch for them because we woke early and fuck through the morning.

I promised to get with them soon and gave them my number had they want to get into acting and possibly a music video. They were more than enthusiastic.

I ate breakfast with them and then went to the hotel desk to get a rental vehicle. The uniformed clerk asked did I want insurance. I paid for the insurance. As I waited for the vehicle to be brought from the garage, I bought a map of the area from the hotel. The vehicle was a 2013 Hummer. I like big vehicles.

I inspected the vehicle and the vehicle was clean of dents and scratches.

The stereo system worked. Everything in the vehicle was in working condition.

I drove a mile from the hotel out of distance and lifted the hood. I disconnected the mileage indicator. Rental agencies calculate the number of miles driven on the vehicle. I save money disconnecting the mechanism.

A Lady Gaga album was in the CD player. I listened to her. A favorite song from her is Poker Face. I skipped to the song and studied the map of Las Vegas.

I visited Las Vegas before, but one never could have enough idea where things were, an I don't want to ask anyone for directions. I don't trust them.

People will give you the wrong directions when asked.

Any learning organization in Las Vegas I consider is the only thing students learn is how to become a card shark and scam gamblers in the casino.

The highway sign to the University of Nevada Las Vegas was glowing in lights as the casinos. A sign at the entrance directed to the administration's office. Hundreds of cars occupied the parking areas with silver covers in the windows keeping the vehicle cooler in hot temperatures.

It was 1:13 P.M. and students make their treks from building to building carrying their materials and backpacks. The buildings were red brick monstrosities scattered over a substantial acreage numbered and lettered.

I followed the directions to the administration's office and asked a mid drift thirty something woman with the complexion of snow white skin who had dark hair, narrow hips in a silver tweed skirt, proportionate round breasts and a pair attractive skinny legs at the information desk could I speak to professor Carl Thomson. She said the professor was absent and asked could a message be relayed to him.

I answered a question with a question and asked her how long will he be gone?

"I really can't say when he'll be here. Perhaps one of the other clerks can tell you. Or perhaps his sister will be able to tell you."

"Where can I find her?"

She typed on the computer at the desk and said," Professor Cecilia Thomson is in building 3C room 101. It's the third building from this building on the right. The buildings are numbered and lettered."

I found the building with her directions and entered into the building where plaques of astonishing scientists hung on the walls. There was Einstein, Benjamin Franklin, and other astonishing photos of profound scientists.

I walked through the halls as any other student does when they begin at the university. Door 101 was easily found and the door was open. An attractive brunette with shoulder length hair in a polyester suit skirt the color of blue sat at the desk of an empty room studying a textbook. She looked up when I stepped into the room.

"May I help you?"

"Are you Professor Cecilia Thomson?"

"I am Professor Cecilia Thomson, and you are?"

"I am looking for Professor Carl Thomson. My name is Martin Hilton."

"I'll tell you the same thing I told the other gentlemen. I don't know where my brother is."

"Things are not what they seem."

"What do you mean?"

"What if your brother Carl didn't run off with her?"

"Are you saying my brother is dead?"

"No. I'm saying something is stale."

"Who are you Mr. Hilton?"

"I am a friend of a friend. Anita Nelson. Mrs. Nelson suggested I could talk with Mrs. Parker and rent her house. I am a producer. I was in need of a place to do a music video. Mrs. Parker met me at the airport yesterday morning."

She waited a moment and got up and closed the door.

My eyes followed her ass, legs, and thighs.

She moved softly; feminine with a determination in her stride.

She had evidently been studying her teacher's manual for I seen the red words which were the answers in the textbook.

Diagrams and phrases were drawn on the chalkboard. Books were neatly arranged on a shelf.

She came to her desk and pulled her chair in front of her desk.

"Have a seat," Ms. Thomson said gesturing to a student's desk in the front row.

I sat at the desk. Ms. Thomson sat in the chair and crossed her legs.

Her lips were pure and sexual with red lipstick. Her face was innocent. Her pale skin was clean of imperfections. Her eyes were attractive and purple.

Her hair was worn like Cleopatra. Cut above her eyes and long around the remainder her head.

"Mr. Hilton my brother was washed up here. If he and that woman skipped out, he had nothing here anyway. My brother Carl was a fool for that woman; another man's wife. Carl said they were in love and they were meant for each other. You can't just engage with another man's wife and expect you can come here again like nothing happen when you work a respectable occupation and the man's wife is in a powerful position as Mr. Parker. Maybe he can make a living in a correspondence school but his life here at the university is over."

"Had your brother Carl and Mrs. Parker been planning on running away together?"

"I would say about the past fifteen days ago, he changed. He was excited about something. He told me he'd make a way for everything to work its way out with Mrs. Parker. I couldn't make him see what an idiot he was for her. He had big dreams before he met her. He arranged his schedule to where he had Wednesdays and Fridays off every week and Tuesday afternoons opened every other week. Carl never had a woman like that. Once she seduced him, he was different," Cecilia said through tears.

"That's life. Don't cry."

"He was hypnotized by what was between her legs. He doesn't give hoots as to what he did to me," Cecilia murmured.

"What do you mean?"

"I never said this to anyone. I love him. I told him he didn't need her. When she seduced him, I and he grew distant. We were lovers. We loved each other. I told him I would give him pussy whenever he wanted. I gave him pussy whenever he wanted. I suck his dick and swallow his spunk. I suck his dick and keep sucking after he squirts in my mouth. Now he wants to squirt in someone else's pussy and not mine. We were there for each other, Mr. Hilton."

"I wish I had a sister to fuck every day. I wouldn't need another woman. I'd squirt in my sister every day."

Her eyes lit up like The Neon Cowboy.

"You would Mr. Hilton?" Cecilia asked.

"We'd have sex whenever my dick got erect. She'd have my baby. I'd keep our relationship quiet and move to another town where no one knows we're related."

Cecilia pulled her top down and her breasts from her bra. Her nipples were large and my nether rod was filling with blood getting erect. She stood and pulled her skirt to the floor. Her cunt was semi hairy. I stood from the desk and pulled my clothes off to my shoes and socks and grabbed her body and sat her on her teacher's desk, opened her legs and slammed my penis in her wet vagina. Her breath was heavy as I moved inside her. She held onto me as she was holding on for dear life; tightly and her head on my neck.

Her nipples pierced my chest. I kissed her neck. I kissed her cheeks. I kissed her lips as I moved inside her womb. Her vaginal fluids spilled. She muffled a sound and I silenced her with my mouth on hers. With each forward movement I made in her she squealed delightfully.

I laid her down flat on the desk, opened her legs wider holding her from her narrow hips, and looked deep in her eyes, penetrating her core. Her legs were limp. I swung her left leg on my shoulder blades rumbling her hips and thighs there on the desk massively reaching her ovaries with my penis. Cecilia climaxes again as I do with her. I couldn't pull out of her pussy. I didn't want to pull out of her pussy. I craved the full effect of orgasm in her pussy; flesh on flesh and came in her pussy. I wailed loud as I reached my pinnacle. Her cunt made my dick explode like no other.

Three

"He thought the world should revolve around their love. He had a nine o'clock seminar on Tuesday. I thought he would get to the university and clean up in the morning. When he didn't attend his seminar, I got uneasy. The Sheriff came today and said his car was found at the airport. I'll need to arrange and get the car, I figure. The manifest says a Mr. and Mrs. Tom Carlson bought tickets to Italy. Airline personnel gave a description fitting Carl and Eloisa at the airport boarding the plane from the continent yesterday at thirty minutes from three p.m."

"Mrs. Parker met me at the airport yesterday, Wednesday. We went to her home up the mountain where she had the house for rent. There was a tree blocking the road. We hiked the way to the house. We were to negotiation the rent. We swam in the pool. She was shot dead in the forehead from a sniper. I ran for help down

the mountain. I came with the Las Vegas
Sheriff to the house and the body was gone.
The blood was gone. Somebody covered
the murder up. The Sheriff thinks Mrs.
Parker staged the scene and skipped town
with your brother. I saw her dead body.
Susceptibly, they didn't get on that airplane
and Eloisa and Carl are dead and her
husband Prentice looks like a promising
contestant for their deaths," I said to Cecilia
as I were in her guts.

Cecilia began to cry.

"Hold on to me. I am here to comfort
you," I murmured through her cries.

She slumped on my body in the
helplessness of sorrow. I held her
massaging her back in that comforting
motion as she buried her head in my
shoulder.

Minutes after, I squirted in her again.

I stood there ten to thirteen minutes in
her womb, holding her.

"Let's get out of here. I'll follow you
home and we can discuss this," I comforted
her.

We dressed and we went from the university. Cecilia Thomson drove an Acura 3.2 TL.

Her home was a spacious red brick house, two bedroom, two bathrooms, chimney, garage home, with a large front and rear yard with a six feet fence surrounding.

We sat in her sitting room. She offered coffee. I declined. I wasn't a coffee wacko craving caffeine each second of the day. I don't wait in Starbucks for coffee with a pistol looking for line jumpers.

"I can't believe Carl is dead. She picked up a picture from an end table next to the couch. "This is my brother Carl. Running away with Eloisa is more logical. What am I going to do?"

She and her brother were smiling and standing in a classroom. His smile was innocent. Carl Thomson was tall, broad shouldered, narrow. He had a complete head of dark brown hair. He wore a tweed brown blazer with patches on the elbows and dark slacks. He looked like an intelligent man who will join a young female student in a sexual relationship.

"You are going to pull together. I'm here for you Cecilia."

"Thank you Mr. Hilton."

"Martin."

"Martin," Cecilia murmured dabbing the tears from her eyes. "They just met about eight months ago. Mr. Parker came to a university fund raiser. Mr. Parker donated seven thousand dollars to the university. Mrs. Parker attended with her husband."

"I think what we need to do is go to the airport, get and check the car. Maybe Carl left a clue or a checklist of his plans."

"Yes, there may be a clue of some sort in his car."

Cecilia stood. She was close to the brink of collapsing into a series of uncontrollable weeps.

Cecilia thought: Maybe Carl left a message on the answering machine.

Cecilia checked the answering machine. She heard the message and I heard the message. I grabbed her before she hit the carpeted floor and carried her to the sofa.

Carl Thomson's body was found in the trunk of his car at the airport parking lot.

"They found his body in the trunk!" Cecilia screamed hysterically. "They killed him. They killed Carl. Who are these people? They probably made him suffer. They probably tied him to a chair, beat him, electrocuted him, shot him in the kneecap and then shot him in the head!"

She stood up.

She paced around the room with her hand to her forehead in agony, sorrow and discuss. I came to her and led her to her bedroom.

"Lie down. Relax. You can't do him any well. He would want you to relax and find his killer."

"This wouldn't have happened if it wasn't for that home wrecker," Cecilia said.

"We will find out who did this Cecilia," I murmured.

"Martin, hold me Martin. Will you stay with me?"

"I'll stay with you Cecilia."

"Hold me and never let me go. Make love to me."

Four

I stayed the night with Cecilia Thomson. The sex was great.

The next morning we rode to the Sheriff station. The station was on the south side of town. There were about twenty cars parked in the parking lot. Some marked and unmarked.

We arrived at the station eight o'clock in the morning.

We walked in to the air-conditioned chill of the station. Immediately a deputy asked, "Do you need help?"

"I came to speak with Sheriff Fickle," Cecilia said.

The deputy looked me over an adverted his eyes to Cecilia. It was the deputy Harry Wheeler.

"Sheriff Fickle is interviewing a suspect and will be out soon. I will let him know you are here to see him Ms. Thomson," Wheeler said.

When Sheriff Fickle came he was assisting a strewed man in a business suit out of an interrogation room. He had a narrow face, deeply socked eyes, and graying hair. He had great confidence as a car salesman. When I heard Fickle say his name, and Cecilia screaming at the man, I knew who he was.

Mr. Parker.

"Your wife got my brother Carl killed!" Cecilia said.

"Carl was way in over his head," Mr. Parker said.

"Mr. Hilton. We meet again. I thought you would have high tailed it out of here," Sheriff Fickle said.

"Las Vegas is interesting," I said.

"So this is Mr. Hilton. I've heard about the great producer. What an honor to meet you Mr. Hilton. Please do come see me when you could. Perhaps I could get you to film a memoir," Mr. Parker said.

"Working with you will be interesting," I said.

"Professor Thomson, sorry for your lose. Pardon me, I have business to tend to," Mr. Parker said.

An officer sprung at the Sheriff with a file folder and he took it and ushered us in the same interrogation room.

***

"Do you think Mr. Parker could be behind this whole thing? After all, he didn't want Carl and Eloisa together. Could Mr. Parker hate Carl enough to want to kill him?" Cecilia asked.

"That doesn't seem likely, knowing that I know Mr. Parker. He loved Eloisa. Sure with Carl gone, that would make him more attractive to Eloisa. Prentice could have chased Carl thousands of miles away, but that wouldn't captivate her mind. Prentice didn't want to lose Eloisa. Eloisa had it in her grasp to crumble Prentice and she didn't because Prentice was her realty. Eloisa was living in a daydream. She had that dream she could get any man and string them along like puppets. When her performance wasn't marvelous and either she didn't get what she want, she would scream, pull her hair, and throw things at Prentice. I know because I came to his homes and casinos when disputes happened. Eloisa made a reputation for attention. Prentice would blow it off because he knew she was a neurotic. Days later Eloisa and Prentice would be hosting social gatherings together and spotted heading into a presidential at a hotel. She'd swear she never thrown a tantrum and acted like it had never happened. Eloisa believed what she wanted to believe. Prentice was her daddy, friend, husband and lover. If Prentice had it in his mind to smash Carl, he would have done so sooner. Prentice knew it wouldn't last. Prentice was just waiting her out," Fickle said.

"Who killed my brother?!" Cecilia yelled.

"I don't know as of now. The forensics team collects Carl was killed in a different place other than his vehicle and his body dumped in the trunk. He was shot in the head. The car was wiped clean of fingerprints. There's no facial recognition.

Carl's body was identified from blood records at the hospital. The body was chopped to pieces and no dental," Fickle said.

Cecilia clamped her hands onto the arms of her chair and thrust her arms out, and dug deep down and yelled, "Find who killed my brother and bring him to me. I'll tear their body from limb to pieces with my bare hands!"

"I am going to comb the globe for the man and woman who took those plane tickets out of here. I am going to find one or both of them. I am going to make them beg for the chance to tell me everything they know about the professor's death and Eloisa's whereabouts, if she is alive. I am going to scope out everybody in this state who owns a gun matching the caliber," Sheriff Fickle said.

"I understand you are upset. We have rules dear lady. I will find who killed the professor and he will be punished properly," Fickle said.

"We'll find who killed Carl, Cecilia," I said cutting into her hostile agitation conversation.

"If anything turns up, I'll contact you at once," Fickle said.

She stood up slowly. She stumbled against me and walked uncertainly toward the door. I stood up and she paused for breath, breathing deeply. "If you don't find who killed my brother, I will," she said.

"I'll find the culprit who did it. Don't worry your pretty self to death," Fickle said.

She opened the door and I steered her to the vehicle. I put her in and I went around and got behind the wheel.

"He will always live in your heart."

I pulled her to me. She huddled into my arms and the sobs came like Niagara Falls.

I could feel the terrible deep sobs as her chest heaved up and down in misery and grief, as she choked up and released her feelings on my shoulders in tears. She had settled into a morbid rhythm; a long time that consisted till she pushed herself away from me. Her hair was matted and her eyes were bloated. She laid the seat back further and touched her head with her hand as to wipe away sweat and tears. Her sobs began again and her hands became as a mask; shielding her emotions from the world.

I started the engine and started to her home.

The sun was far from drifting to the other side of the globe. In Las Vegas, the show lights remained on in all spectacular. They reassured the livelihood of the city.

Every few seconds a sob would shake her like a bolt of electricity.

I pulled in her driveway and escorted her inside. She clung on my body as a shark a shade of gray clamping on a human.

I held her in my arms.

She kissed me.

She was aware of her actions.

She required the comfort and the desire to be needed by the opposite sex.

Her kisses became her unclothing--me unclothing--to our union of sex.

She was free from her condemnation of her brother's death as I was inside her. Whether she imagined I was he, I did not know.

After our sex we sleep and I awoke to preparing provisions. We showered and she made love to me again and we sleep once more.

Five

I arrived at the Parker place at ten forty.
Fickle was kind providing me with the
whereabouts of Mr. Parker. The house was
large almost like a castle. For at the gate I
could look upon the house. I pressed the
intercom button.

"Mr. Hilton here to meet a Mr. Parker."

No more than three seconds passed and
a voice answered, "Mr. Hilton I am
expecting you. The gates will open. Please
drive in," Mr. Parker said.

The gates opened and I drove in.

I was on a business aventurine more
rather than looking in to the location of
Mrs. Parker. Thy querying on her
whereabouts was nearly a topic I would
bring to the surface. I wasn't going to
converse I had sex with a married woman
and her husband was a potential client.

"The servants are not live-ins. They're
pesky when one is of knead of privacy.
They are hired day to day," Mr. Hilton said.

As Mr. Parker led me to his sitting room filled with leather furniture, hundreds of books, a mini bar, and a fireplace, he offered me a drink.

"I do not drink alcoholic drinks. These bottles appear an imported scotch or liquor--no these are the purest grape juices," Mr. Parker said. "Owning casinos and drinking alcohol is not a wise option. It's a no brainer. You drink, you get impaired and you throw money at things and people you wouldn't consider. You sober and you sober poorer."

I took a glass of grape juice. It was really delicious. I guessed he did not intend it was the purest meaning a guy in rubber boots squished the grapes in a barrel and bottled it.

Mr. Parker seated in a leather chair. He wore a tailored gray suit and polished leather shoes. He gave the impression of Hue Heffner at the Playboy mansion. I was expecting the Playboy Bunnies to come through with giggles and bouncing breasts asking me who boobs look realer? Had they come through, I'd grope each breast, tell them I could only say when I slide dick in them and see their breasts bounce during intercourse before giving an answer.

The Playboy Bunnies where not there and I made a mental note to contact the sisters from the hotel room.

"Each day I go to the casino and I see gamblers. Poker--One card can change the game. You get a great hand and you flinch, and your opponent knows you possess a great hand and he folds. You can't get him to up the ante. You're holding a pair to his three of a kind. You up the jackpot bluffing him. If your palms are not sweaty and you put on a great poker face, trying not to flinch your eyes or let your eyes graze across the casino avoiding direct eye contact, maybe he won't become aware you are bluffing and just maybe he knows you're bluffing and getting you to raise the pot. Professionals. Card sharks. Las Vegas is full of them. Wear sun glasses. Hide your eyes when playing poker. Don't make repeat body motions or tapping on the table. Don't tap your foot when you possess a great hand or a not so great hand. Poker is like chess and you are the chess piece. You make one wrong move and the game is over. Your only change at a stalemate is to leave the casino with the amount you came with and nothing less. There really is no stalemate. Gas expense. Food. Time consumed. You're emotions are stirred. You had fun didn't you, gambling? Fun? Can you put a price on fun? Can you put a reasonable price on fun? Everybody has their price whether in cash, or fun or another object. Everything has a price. My wife had a price and she spent money easily. She spent money with him. The professor."

"Is that why the professor is dead? Who killed him?"

"The professor is dead because his life was the price of being with another woman's wife. He died because he was in a not so happy place for him. I didn't kill him. I know who did."

"Who killed him?"

"A murderer." Mr. Parker began to laugh.

Very hilarious. Mr. Parker was a big deal in casinos. He was laughing at a man's death. He was, to the people, evil. Evil greets evil and evil knocks at everyone's door.

"In the world I live in, power is centralized by money. Wealth. It goes against my grain to place myself in a position as such labeled as a murderer. Look around you Mr. Hilton. I own large estates and casinos. Greed can make any human murder. Love can make any human murder and crumble and the professor crumbled. I don't crumble. My wife used him up. Why I wouldn't be surprised my wife is dead buried in the lands of Nevada. I loved her dear is why I wouldn't give her a divorce. She would come to reality I was the greater man for her. She was a bunny in her emotions. Quick, feisty and a darn marvelous love maker. She did not care for an anchor weighting her down all her life. She was as any young girl. Hot in her cunt. As of her father's estate, it was dry as an oil drill in Texas spurting up dust."

"Why are you telling me this?"

"So that we have an understanding if we are going to oblige in business. I am a businessman. You are here on business."

I was here on business. I thought a many of thoughts, who cares if Mrs. Parker got shot? I don't. I'm not a detective. I'm not a cop. I'm not a private investigator. What do I look like risking my life trying to find out if a stranger is dead or skipped town with her lover? I'm not wasting my life looking for her. She'd dead. Or she's flown the coop with Carl Thomson. I'm alive. The sniper wasn't shooting at me. What's in Vegas stays in Vegas. Move on with my business and live forward.

The super hero thought of finding Cecilia brother's killer impulse a thought into my mind that I could find the killer and Cecilia an I could begin a long term relationship and she'll forever cling to me; as a modern day slave. A sex slave. Cecilia clung to me now as an infant baby clings to a dirty diaper waiting to be changed.

I was in a web of love. What a weave is web.

I leaned back in the leather chair opposite him.

He raised.

"Will you care for another drink?" He said.

"No."

He made his way to the bar, replenished his drink and came slowly back to the leather chair opposite me.

"Mr. Hilton I would like this memoir to decorate my broad sense of character and integrity. I would like this documentary to go viral. To captivate the young entrepreneur and say, 'You too can climb the ladder and become successful. Hard work, determination and more of all the ingredient of passion'. Passion Mr. Hilton accommodated with a thrive can lead to the top. Guess what is at the top."

"Money."

"You are a business man Mr. Hilton."

"That I am Mr. Parker."

He lifted up out of the chair and went over next to the bar where a large portrait of him hung.

I understood why the portrait was not over the fireplace. I lived in a mansion and when the logs are kindling, a portrait above the mantel piece will get hot and damaged. It is a fire hazard.

He pressed a hidden button under the frame and the portrait swung open like a door. There was a square wall safe built into the wall. He stepped in front and turned the dial. I heard the dial as he turned it. I pondered in my mind what the combination is, when he is not at home, and how much cash money was in the hidden safe. I pushed those thoughts from my mind. An alarm system wouldn't stop me from going in the safe as it wouldn't stop anybody else from going in the safe. Pull out the electric meter and the power goes off. If there was a backup power generator, I'd have the combination to get inside the safe quicker.

I pushed the thoughts out of my mind. It would be another addition to somebody who murdered his wife and his wife's mistress. It'll be perfect to accommodate his present situation and me getting richer.

I set aside the scheme of robbing his rich ass whether I was tuning my ears to hear the clinks of the dial for the combination and looking at his hand movement as he did at the safe.

When he closed the safe and spun the dial he came back to the chair and flipped a stack of money in my hand and took a seat.

"That is $5,000 for getting started on the video memoir to get your equipment here and set things up."

"Mr. Parker thank you for your business."

I put the stack of money into the inside pocket of my blazer.

I did not want to give the impression I was running with the money. I did not possess enough camera equipment with me for this travel and take to the making of his video memoir. From the ear of things, Mr. Parker will enjoy his memoir on film as a commercial or a campaign advertisement for political office. He was paying an I will record. I will also encourage higher rates for my services. He did not ask a price an I did not tell him a definite price. He would know no difference. He was flinging money around and his wife is dead.

"Mr. Parker, my device of this minute is a portable camera I carry with me for quick photos and video. I must contact my workers for the arrival of the equipment for such a large job."

"I intend you will be quick about this in a professional manner."

"I will contact my workers today. I do have this camera and I will take pictures. With technology I can enhance or deplete any facial calamity you see fit for your image."

"Technology is a genius," Mr. Parker personified in a clever monotone.

He stared at me and for a second I witnessed the eyes of a business man or a murderer and what man in business didn't tell lies or murder? Mainly a business man does either. The neither is a foreigner or comes from a rich family. Take show biz for example. Many of the actors on the television are the spawn of producers, other successful actors, singers, or business men and women.

I didn't care to stay in the place alone with him when I didn't know for certain he killed his wife and her heart throb professor. I took a dozen set of photos and asked him did he like any changes in his image. He bluntly stated, "Make me look ten years younger." I said I could.

As he opened the door I came through, he said, "When you film, make the words appear at the bottom of the screen like the Chinese karate movies."

I said I'll include the closed caption and made my way to the vehicle.

I waited till I drove from the estate and contacted my camera crew. I pulled into the Peppermill Restaurant & Fireside Lounge. I awaited a double steak entree, sitting at a table for one.

I phoned my crew. They said they will schedule a flight for tomorrow.

With the camera crew there with me working on Mr. Parker's video diary, I wouldn't feel comfortable in the same room with him. Had he not been a possible suspect, perhaps I could've felt at ease, but no. He was a business tycoon and business tycoons were aggravatingly pressuring for money.

They're really beggars.

The steak could've had more flavors and I made my opinion to the server and the owner of the establishment. The owner gave me fifteen percent off the steak.

While I was there at the diner I wondered could Mrs. Parker's former maid give anything to help. I searched The White

Pages on the internet of my iPhone and found a number and address of Mayumi Jade.

I phoned her. Told her I was a friend of Mrs. Parker and asked may I come talk to her? She agreed.

Six

I found the resident of Mayumi Jade not too far from the mansion of Mr. Parker. It was a large house of shutters painted white with brown lining.

The sidewalk was neatly trimmed. The grass was manicured and the shrubbery was eight feet away from the foundation. The neighboring house was three hundred feet away as the others houses were in the neighborhood.

Mayumi Jade opened the door on the third ring of the doorbell. She was in her mid twenties, black long shinny hair to the middle of her back, pale and sexy. She wore a red knee high dress and leather red sandals. Her feet were pretty. Her legs were attractive.

"You are Mr. Hilton the man I spoke with on the phone?"

"I am Mr. Hilton."

"Do come in."

The furniture was white leather, the house extraordinarily clean. I was glad the house didn't look like the home of a hoarder. Each piece of furniture was eight feet apart for comfort.

Mayumi Jade knew how to decorate.

Furniture crammed together was tacky and unorthodox. One needed space for moving. Each door should open completely. No door should be blocked. No objects should be around the doorways. A distance of arm length at the minimum is proper for closeness of surrounding objects. In pathways a proper distance from surrounding objects should begin at arm length.

Walking through a home or any place stretching arms and touching objects is hoarding. Nobody wants to knock things down walking through doorways and pathways or bumping things because your furniture is too close together.

"Have a seat."

I took a seat in a red velvet love seat. Mayumi Jade sat on the matching red velvet couch and crossed her legs.

"I'd like to talk to you about Mr. Parker. I am a friend of a friend and I am hired by Mr. Parker as a producer of his memoir on video."

"Is he ill?"

"No. He is well. I wouldn't know where to begin other than Mrs. Parker is dead and the professor Carl Thomson is dead. There is suspicion Mr. Parker killed them or hired to kill them. The professor's body was found in a trunk. His wife's body has yet to be found."

"I am not surprised. If O.J. Simpson could get off murdering his wife and her boyfriend so can Mr. Parker."

"Mr. Parker is only suspected and is a rumor. Ms. Thomson, Carl's sister, believes Mr. Parker hired somebody or killed them," I said.

"Mr. Parker loved Eloisa. Eloisa and Prentice got along well together. Eloisa loved Carl. Eloisa said Carl treated her like a real woman. Prentice was older than Eloisa and Prentice treated her like a wife and a daughter. Prentice and Eloisa did love each other. Eloisa was young and not ready for a commitment of marriage. It's really none of my business. I just wish people to stop coming by my home bothering me about Mr. Parker and Mrs. Parker."

"Mrs. Parker was your friend."

"Mrs. Parker was not my friend. I was just a maid."

"Mrs. Parker told me you frequently talked."

"I was there when she babbled on about her husband and her boyfriend. I couldn't help but listen. That's why I am not a maid anymore. I don't want to hear about someone else's life. I don't want to hear that crappy every day. Just because I was a maid doesn't mean I'm a marriage counselor or a mentor."

"Do you know anyone who may have killed them? Do you know anybody Mr. Parker worked with who may have killed them?"

"I know Mr. Parker's associates. I know more about Mr. Parker than his wife did," Mayumi said easily.

"How do you know them?" I asked.

"I know them because I had sex with them and Mr. Parker."

Mayumi uncrossed her legs. She rubbed the length of her legs an up to her warm wet spot in the middle of her thighs. She stood and came and stood in front of me. She lifted her red skirt. She sat down on my lap. My hands automatically took to her body.

"This is what Mr. Parker's associates desired," Mayumi sexily murmured and reached an unzipped my trousers. She pulled my third leg from position and murmured, "This is what I desired," referring to my man meat as she held me in her hand. She pulled my pants to my ankles and tasted my cock in one deep gulp and placed me inside of her womb.

Mayumi Jade pulled her skirt top up over her head. Her breasts possessed dark nipples. I grappled each breast. She jousted up and down as she was a cowgirl riding a horse from an episode of Bonanza.

Mayumi Jade balanced her cunt on my penis using the back end of the couch for leverage as she slammed her vagina on my sex with her feet buried in the seat of the cushions. Each force of my sex meeting its peak in her womb brought out a high pitch squeal of delight. The eroticism of her oriental flesh made our union much more special and sexual. She smacked her wet love canal on my shaft and came. Her fluids no doubly flooded to the cushion.

She was a former maid so unsuspectingly she could clean the stains of the erratic fucking. Her sperm bank was expecting a donation an I pulled her down on my love stick and held her there and made my deposit of sperm.

Mayumi Jake was so attractive and I was not satisfied sexually with one orgasm. She invited my trouser snake it was what she is getting. I laid her on the couch and pulled her skirt off. Her pleasure paradise glistened with juices. I entered in her. Her legs clasped together around my torso as I moved inside her with my own desire of squirting my spunk inside her as I kiss her lips, as her hands caress my back, as I explode my liquid pears in her ocean of pleasure.

Twenty odd minutes later I reached my pinnacle and came inside her narrow hip body and relaxed my love muscle in her many more minutes.

It was awkward after we had sex questioning Mayumi of Mr. Parker, I thought. After sex should be pleasant and calming. Again the thought, why I was inquiring of Mr. Parker and I was not a detective? Mayumi Jade asked a similar question and I replied, "I've been hired by Mr. Parker and I think I should be made aware of the possible dangers of such clients and I was with his wife when she was shot down from a professional sniper."

"Mr. Parker did not build his empire solo. Mr. Parker's lifelong business acquaintance Spurn Castle date from more than thirty years ago. Spurn and Prentice used to buy out small businesses and real estate property and turn profits on the investment. Who they couldn't get on their side they murdered and purchased their property through auction houses. It's speculation of course. They were shoulder to should in business adventures. Spurn and Mr. Parker scratch each other's back to this day. They play poker together in the casinos. Mr. Parker, Spurn Castle, Rip Seep, Tony Richard, and Edward Shoe. The biggest tycoons in Las Vegas. They each watch each other. They're the fabulous five of Las Vegas. They live the slogan 'What happens in Vegas stays in Vegas'. You don't think one of the fabulous five killed his wife and her boyfriend do you? I did not ever overhear any word of Mr. Parker plotting to assassinate his wife and her boyfriend."

"Do you think Spurn Castle would keep Mrs. Parker quiet if Mr. Parker couldn't keep her quite?"

"He would I believe. He and Mr. Parker benefit the largest and they own the biggest casinos in Las Vegas Mr. Hilton."

"Mrs. Parker said two men came by asking about Mr. Parker and his finances. Do you know who they were?"

I was pushing too many questions. Mayumi stared at me an answered, "They were auditors. Mrs. Parker was threatening Mr. Parker to give her more money and Mr. Parker said her father's money was zilch. The thousands of money she received from her husband was not enough for her."

"Thank you Mayumi."

"Do you care to stay for another round of sex?"

I could not say no to that an I wouldn't. I stayed and she massaged my penis with her vagina. Mayumi offered food and I declined. Las Vegas was unusual and I couldn't trust her too far. Sex and a meal and the Las Vegas motto was a thought I did not care to think about.

I drove twenty minutes and drove in at a restaurant and parked. I phoned Cecilia and asked how she was holding up. She said she was better. She did not look better. Video conversations were great. One could see the human on the other end of the conversation. Dried streams of tears lined her face. I said I was researching into who killed her brother. It gave her relief she had help on her side from the tone in her voice. I did not tell her Mr. Parker hired me for his video memoir. It would've upset her and she would feel she had no one on her side.

I asked my iPhone for the information of the top contenders in Las Vegas. Sure enough Spurn Castle, Rip Seep, Tony Richard, Edward Shoe and Mr. Prentice Parker were the top five in Las Vegas. I saved each contact number an address to a folder labeled Fabulous Five on my iPhone.

I made my way into the restaurant. A flat screen television was set on the north wall of the restaurant. The tables were seated around the establishment and the center was a dance floor. Eight electronic slot machines were cast off to the west in a separate room. I could see them easily when I made way through the front door.

I ordered a gigantic steak and a glass of orange juice. After I ate I left a two dollar and twenty-five cent tip because the sexy large breast narrow hip brunette waitress plopped her boobs out and gave me a show. If the waitress did not show her big white breasts I'd not tipped her. If the waitress showed her cunt I'd tipped her another twenty-five cents. I wasn't going to tip anybody more than two dollars and fifty cents.

My Spiderman spider senses were tingling and I seated in the Humvee and drove to the residence of Cecilia.

Cecilia met me at the door with a hug and a kiss on the lips.

"I need you," Cecilia murmured.

I pulled her closer. We swayed silently. She pulled me to her bedroom. She was wearing a Las Vegas night shirt the length of her knees. She pulled her shirt up and worked her fingers around the buckle of my pants and I stepped from them and I pulled my shirt off and placed my hands around her naked body and kissed her lips passionately. Her arms moved around my shoulders and I carried her the steps to the bed, laid her down and entered her.

My cock disappeared into her love canal. She pulled me closer. Her breasts were pressed against my chest. I kissed her lips. She spread wide her legs and clasped them around my body. She smiled. I knew desire. I knew passion.

I knew the building pressure inside had to be released. I helped her release that pressure as I moved inside her. Her fingers splayed against my back. Her fingers threaded through my hair. Her fingers caressed my neck tenderly. She repressed the memory of how cold blooded the world was around her with my sex. She gasps as she reached a sexual peak and her juices flowed forth her womb.

I made a wail of a sigh and I ferociously kissed her lips as our bodies meets in the steamiest intercourse and I squirted in her cum dump.

Cecilia slept the night in my warm embrace.

In the morning I awaken to the ring tone of Lady Gaga, 'Applause'.

I answered the iPhone. It was my camera crew. They were at the airport. I showered. I dressed. Cecilia put down some victuals at the kitchen table.

I didn't know how Cecilia will react to me working with the man who possibly killed her brother or hired a hit man to silence his life forever, so I didn't tell her.

I said to her I had to go conduct business. I will return to her when finished.

I kiss her and climbed in the seat of the Humvee and drove to the airport.

The airport was on the north side of the city. The terminal looked like a mini casino. Slot machines lined the seating area for soon to be passengers.

My camera crew consisted of three crew members.

The three were women.

Sheila Diamond had shinny black hair reaching the length midway of her back.

Her eyes were blue. Her complexion was pale and smooth. She was twenty nine and her breasts were spectacular--size 29 C cup. Her hips were narrow and her legs were smooth and sexy.

My Japanese camerawoman Yui Ching was twenty one. I love her narrow hips--her black silky shinny hair to her hips--her red eyes--pale oriental skin complexion--her sexy legs and creamy thighs and her 29 double C size breasts.

Paris Nimbler was twenty three. She was Irish decent. Her dark brunette hair to her narrow hips, her blue eyes, 39 double C breasts, and sexy smooth legs made her features and qualifies her as a hot sexy woman.

The three women roused the snake in my trousers when I laid eyes on them at the airport.

In the airport lounge I told them I had met Eloisa at her house in the mountains and had witnessed her death and Mr. Parker hired me to make record of his accomplishments. Their responses were mutual. Sheila, Yui, and Paris insisted we have sex before a hit man comes for me.

And get the memoir made and get out of
Las Vegas alive. I agreed I didn't want to
stay around. We checked into a hotel and
fucked liked it was our last chance to fuck
again.

Paris was a professional dick sucker.
She knew how to suck a dick; no hands. I
drove my love stick in their narrow hips
like I drove that SUV fleeing from the
sniper; nonstop.

Paris suckled Yui's pussy as I dived in
Paris' cunt an asshole. Paris suckled Sheila's
insides as I squirted in the anal and cunt of
Paris.

Sheila licked Yui's insides as I anal
fucked Sheila and fucked her cunt and
released hot semen in Sheila.

Yui licked Sheila and Paris insides as I
fucked Yui in her openings and reached my
pinnacle.

We rotated.

I didn't lick their cunt. I didn't believe
in slurping a woman's vagina. I never did
suckle a woman's fetus flaps and I wasn't
going to begin ever.

They licked each other's genitalia to
orgasms an I inserted my cock in them

when they were the most wet; lubricated
with the orgasmic fluids.

Seven

At 10:30 A.M. two days after my camera crew arrived and we fucked two complete days, we came to the mansion of Mr. Parker.

I didn't set easy working with a murder suspect. The cash money helps tremendously.

Mr. Parker appraised my lovely attractive camerawomen and congratulated me.

"You have excellent taste Mr. Hilton," Mr. Parker had said.

We went straight to business. We finished recording in three days.

I told my crew I needed to go visit a friend before I left.

I seated in the Hummer and drove to Cecilia.

She was not there.

I pulled the Hummer in the driveway and I found the spare key Cecilia had made for me on my key ring. I fitted the key in the lock and went in.

Perhaps she left a note telling me when she would be back.

I saw no note. I smelled a distinctive vapor in the air. Gun oil. I knew it from working on the movie set of an Arnold Schwarzenegger movie in Hollywood some years back. I saw a receipt for a gun sale in a draw where the lamp sat at in her bedroom. Cecilia had seen the campaign commercials I figured and now more than likely she will go kill Mr. Parker.

I picked up the phone receiver and dialed the Sheriff. He was not there and I relayed my suspicions of an attempt on Mr. Parker's life.

Eight

**Cecilia stared down at the .45 caliber
in her hand**--the silver handle--the metallic
shaft to the nozzle--an envisioned Mr.
Parker fallen to his death from the fatal
gunshot wound when she pulled the trigger.

Cecilia had seen Mr. Parker on
television announcing he was campaigning
for Governor. He was having a press
conference in the park and arena twenty
nine days after the remains of her brother
Carl were discovered in the trunk of his
own car. That day was today.

Cecilia seated into the seat, admitting
to herself that this will not be the end of her
sorrow, only a milestone to revenge the
death of her brother.

She turned the key in the ignition and
pulled away from the driveway.

She drove a moderate speed limit to the
strip. She parked her car in a free hotel lot
and took a ride on the Las Vegas Monorail.
The Monorail stopped at resorts and the

convention facilities. When the Monorail stopped at the Las Vegas Convention Center she ventured to the restroom and boarded again to complete her mission.

Cecilia got off of the Monorail and made her way to the campaign area.

The Las Vegas strip park and arena was finally completed. It was a new idea to get visitors to Las Vegas and welcome more gamblers. It counters to casinos historic strategy of trying to keep people inside of casinos buying more chips and flitting to one gamble attraction to the next.

Modern visitors like darting in and out of lounges, bars, clubs, casinos and the popular events. Now people have a place to enjoy fresh air outside from the attracting glamorous lights to coerce you to spend more indoors.

Tourists are able to stroll over a replica of the Brooklyn Bridge and the arena seats 20,000. People are able to buy an upscale burger and fries and the traditional soda pops in glass bottles. They could buy complete meals from the restaurant vendors and eat outside on a bench in the park. They could frequent outdoor concerts. It brought great business to the Las Vegas strip, the casinos, and the city of Las Vegas.

The Las Vegas Park an arena was one crowded area two blocks long. Security personnel strolled the area keeping close eye for people who possessed terrorist attacks. There was a group of teenagers with a portable radio on listening to One Direction, the volume turned to a dial that you could hear the vocals clear about a half mile away. Cecilia had seen security talking to teens and steered in the other direction and headed to the arena where Mr. Parker will hold his campaign speeches.

Minutes into Mr. Parker's speech she made her way closest to him and began firing.

Bullets rippled his body. Blood gushed from his head and body--and from the veins and arteries of his throat.

He fell onto his knees, his face absolutely blank, reached a slow hand up to his head, then fell heavily onto the ground.

Security contained Cecilia and took her into the station.

Nine

The airport was crowded and every television channel was turned to the death of Mr. Parker. He was a popular man in Las Vegas.

I seated with my camera crew awaiting flight.

Less than an hour later we were in the skies.

I suggested we stay in separate hotel rooms for our safety.

I rode a cab to the hotel room.

As I approached the hotel clerk taking notice of establishment, the assortment of decorations and the orderly cleanness of the interior, the woman at the service desk said hello and welcome to the La Scalinatella. Her features impressed me at once. She was of middle age, and she was remarkably good-looking. She was tall. Her skin was clear and smooth. She were well endow with a big bosom. Her hips were narrow.

Her features were sexual that at once gave me an erection.

She smiled as she introduced herself while she held out her hand. I clasped that soft snowflake.

Her name was Marla.

To my inquiries she said that she could give me a sitting and bedroom and kitchen. As I looked at her smooth black hair, and cool blue eyes, I felt an hour would not permit before she was mounting the length of my penis.

I led myself to the hotel room.

The floors were polished marble and majolica, with details in wrought iron and gold.

The room opened out onto a private terrace with the view of the sea. The light filled and poured through the immense floor to ceiling windows.

Minutes later after I showered and lie on the bed there was a series of raptures on the door. I answered. It was the desk clerk Marla. She rolled in a trolley full of provisions. Milk and butter with home-made scones, fresh eggs and bacon and coffee from Starbucks.

Marla was beautiful in the erotic sense, her complexion being white and creamy. Red lipstick and her black hair was pure sexy.

She had informed me, she was quite experienced in the art of sex.

I looked into her blue eyes; fathomless blue eyes these were, I absorbed her willpower and made her my abject slave.

I grabbed her body and pulled her closer and caressed her body and removed her clothing fingering her cunt. I laid her on the bed and I pushed forth my member in her wet love canal. A faint sigh rose from her lips. Twenty minutes or more I released my liquid pearls inside her and then I slowly withdrew my dick from her moist cave, entering her asshole.

Twenty more minutes later I reached my sexual pinnacle.

I relaxed on the bed and she swallowed my dick and my scrotum sac and I were of great pleasure.

I cannot recall any when her hands were applied as she was sucking my cock.

I cannot describe her technique other than she did not make of her involvement of her hands on a sexual pleasure which requires no hands; and I only know that from the first lick on my cock, she was a professional.

To lead in words; she was remarkable.

I thought of Cecilia when I was inside of Marla.

From what I learned later I was able to piece together what happened to Eloisa and Professor Carl.

Eloisa sat in Sheriff Fickle's office. She was seated and handcuffed in front of her body. Sheriff Fickle questioned her after they found her running away from the rooftop of the arena. Security heard multiple gunshots other than from where Cecilia fired from the crowds.

Eloisa wrote those tax people. She told them everything she could about her father's money and everything she could about her husband's finances. They said they would investigate. It would've been years before she could get her hands on the money her father stowed for her. She knew I was coming and she planned the staged murder at the pool. She knew she needed someone to see her supposedly get shot.

Without a body and the hired actors on the airplane, it gave her a chance to stage her husband's death. Shooting him at the arena wasn't the plan. He was to die in a home invasion. When Mr. Parker hired me, that changed things. She did not know he was running for Governor.

Why didn't she hire someone to kill Mr. Parker? The Sheriff asked.

She wanted to pull the trigger that killed the wretched old man.

What about Carl Thomson? Didn't she love him? The Sheriff queried.

She loved Carl. Carl wanted to run away together. She knew she did not love him enough to live the rest of her life with him forever. And she didn't trust him. She thought when she received her father's and a large amount of money from Prentice's insurance policy, she believed Carl would hire a hit man for her, is why she hired a hitman to kill him, Eloisa had admitted to Sheriff Fickle.

Fickle gave me the complete details after I called him from a throw away burner phone.

Caboose

Thirty nine days succumbed since I visited Las Vegas and meet Mrs. Eloisa Parker. She is serving a three year sentence for the assault on Mr. Parker and wounding a civilian in the crowd.

Marla and I passed our time engaging in idle sex. Each day we sex. Each night we sex. Her white glowing face, her steadfast blue eyes, those moist pinkish lips, made my dick solid whenever I looked at her. Each morning before work at the hotel I rose and piloted my shaft in her cunt. Her hair enveloped us both like an inky cloud while I lay beneath her as she straddled my dick.